Rory's Piratical Leg

Boys

IAN WHYBROW

ILLUSTRATED BY MARK BEECH

For my friends in the Hope family, for Elizabeth's Legacy of Hope, and in particular for Miss Pollyanna Hope who has the remarkable (and piratical) spirit of the Aurora Hope she inspired ...

Text copyright © 2014 Ian Whybrow
Illustrations copyright © 2014 Mark Beech
First published in Great Britain in 2014
by Hodder Children's Books

The rights of Ian Whybrow and Mark Beech to be identified as the Author and Illustrator of the Work have been asserted by them in accordance with the Copyright, Designs and Patents Act 1988.

1

A Catalogue record for this book is available from the British Library

ISBN 978 1 444 91577 8

Printed and bound in Great Britain by CPI Group (UK) Ltd, Croydon, CR0 4YY

The paper and board used in this paperback by Hodder Children's Books are natural recyclable products made from wood grown in sustainable forests. The manufacturing processes conform to the environmental regulations of the country of origin.

Hodder Children's Books
A division of Hachette Children's Books
338 Euston Road, London NW1 3BH
An Hachette UK company
www.hachette.co.uk

Rory's Dittybox

According to Aunt Smoother, Aurora Hope was lucky. It was true, her aunt admitted, that at the age of three she had lost both her parents in a stagecoach accident … and her right leg. A highwayman had robbed the passengers and then fired his pistol. The horses had bolted and the stagecoach had turned over.

Still, according to Aunt, at least Aurora had family to take care of her.

"Tuh," thought Rory. That was what she called herself. She hated being called Aurora.

Her "family" was made up of Aunt Smoother, Aunt Awful and Uncle Buckup, Rory's guardians. Really, they were only second cousins (twice removed) to her papa, Captain Christopher Hope, but they insisted that she call them Aunt Susan, Aunt Ada and Uncle Barnaby. Rory's only comfort was to have her own secret names for them, tucked away in her head.

Aunt Smoother was a housemaid.

She worked fourteen hours a day up at the Big House. It was her habit to sweep anything that upset her under the carpet.

"Isn't it fortunate that we are allowed to live so very comfortably on a splendid houseboat? Is there not a view of a beautiful mansion set in its own beautiful parkland?" She paused to smooth the blanket that lay across Rory's lap. The girl sat in her wheelchair on deck, looking silently and miserably at the river.

Aunt Smoother ran a brush through Rory's tangled red hair.

"Ouch! Don't be so silly!" thought Rory. She never complained out loud but she knew they were thinking "if only we had been left a handy boy to look after. But a girl with one leg is nothing but a burden to us".

As for the houseboat, it was damp and cold, so leaky and rotten that it was a miracle it was still afloat.

Rory reached for the key that was hanging round her neck on its silver chain. It was said to be the key to her father's sea-chest – his "dittybox" – but that had long since disappeared. Now the key and the blanket her mother had woven for her when she was little were all that was left to remind her of lost happiness.

Meeting Fishface

"What about a little walk today, my precious?" cooed Aunt Smoother. "Just for Auntie."

The crabby voice of Aunt Awful boomed from downstairs. Fourteen hours a day she was cook to the Big House, but the houseboat's galley was her kingdom. "Aurora can go ashore on her crutch and make herself useful! She can take herself off to the tavern and get us a jug of gin!"

"That's the ticket! Shift yourself, Aurora," puffed Uncle Buckup. He had been toiling all day in the garden of the Big House, so he smelled like cheese. "You'll feel right as rain for it. And Mrs Blaggard is coming down from the Big House after supper to make her monthly inspection. We must offer her something to keep her sweet."

Suddenly Rory had had enough. "I shan't," she said fiercely. "I hate Mrs Blaggard, I hate it when you all get drunk, I'm too young to buy alcohol and I am never using that beastly crutch AGAIN!"

"Wicked, ungrateful little monster!" called Aunt Awful, bashing about the galley with her broom. "You'll come to a shocking bad end, you will!"

"I'll fetch Starter!" announced Uncle Buckup, and disappeared below.

Just then, a filthy, ragged boy in a small painted boat rowed under the bow of the houseboat and gave a cheery wave. He made two clicks with his tongue and called out: "All right, Fluffbuttocks?"

This was so unexpected that Rory almost burst out laughing. She had to shout back to stop herself.

"How dare you call me Fluffbuttocks!" she scolded. "I was addressin' your doggy, actually," said the boy, waggling his eyebrows.

Jim, Rory's bouncy springer spaniel, was up from his cushion in a trice, wagging his tail and bristling with excitement. Rory looked down again and noticed a funny little terrier whizzing round in circles on a coil of rope in the bottom of the rowing boat, wagging his tail like mad. The boy gave one oar a tweak, so as to pull right alongside the houseboat and add the words: "Don't flatter yourself, Droopy-drawers."

"Sauce!" squealed Rory with delight, clapping her fingers across her mouth. She leaned over the rail to get a closer look at him and his dog in the late afternoon sun. The boy was grimy, and his clothes were in tatters, but that face had a broad grin on it and the green eyes were bright and lively as his pup's. She had never seen a boy so full of life.

"Take no notice," urged Aunt Smoother. "He's just a rough and silly river-boy. Get away, boy … "

"Well, I like him!" said Rory defiantly, and she called after the boy as he pushed off and away from the side of the houseboat, "Goodbye, Bat-Ears! Mud-Shuffler!"

"My friends call me Fishface," said the boy with a chuckle, gathering speed as he guided the boat into the rising tide and slipped away.

Jim gave a whine of disappointment, as Rory leant over the rail and watched the visitor disappear. "Goodbye, Fishface," she murmured.

There was a whistle in the air behind her, a thwack and a dreadful, stinging pain!

"Bang on target, my old Starter!" cried Uncle Buckup.

Jim sprang up, growled and tried to sink his teeth into his trouser leg, but Uncle Buckup kicked him aside.

"It's all right, Jim," said Rory. The brave little dog grumbled but stood back. Rory didn't cry out, though the stroke of the cane hurt like mad. Instead she spun round, pulled herself straight against the rail and looked her attacker right in the eye. "Give me the jug," she said quietly. "But don't you EVER hit me again."

The Great Escape

When Rory and Jim returned, the
sinking sun had turned the river red
and Mrs Blaggard was seated at the
scrubbed table on deck. She was a
stiff woman, dressed in black from
her buttoned-up boots to her
bonnet; she sat up straight, her
sharp nose swinging accusingly
from side to side like a
weathervane. The aunts and uncle
stood by silently, heads bowed.

As Rory stumbled across the gangplank, Uncle Buckup stepped up smartly towards her. He tipped his head to look in the jug, snatched it from her with one hand and swiped the back of her head with the other.

"She's spilled half of it!" he groaned. "I'm so sorry, Mrs Blaggard."

Mrs Blaggard let out a great impatient sigh and began to speak to no one in particular. "You complain of rotten boards and a window falling out. You demand paint and varnish. You expect repairs."

Nobody spoke.

"I must remind you that my husband and I are not yet the owners of Ailing Estate. We were housekeeper and butler to Lady Ailing until she sold the place. When she died, we became its keepers. Her wishes were that we should remain its keepers for ten years – or until the new owners came. To that end, she left us a small allowance to keep the house and grounds in order. A very small allowance. At the end of this month, our ten years' wait to become owners here will be up. And if nobody comes a-knocking and shows us deeds signed and sealed … which they won't … Ailing House legally becomes Blaggard House.

So you just wait till then before you come whining to me about repairs."

"Very good, Mrs Blaggard," mumbled Uncle Buckup.

If only the real owners would come back, Rory wished. And send these beastly keepers away.

"Ahoy!" came a voice from ten feet down in the water.

Rory looked over the side and saw the boy in a painted rowing boat, holding up a flickering lantern in the twilight. "Fishface!" she cried. He had come back!

In an instant, she made up her mind. She picked up Jim and dropped him over the side, calling, "Catch!"

"Blimey!" said the boy. But he

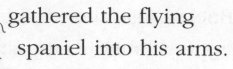

gathered the flying
spaniel into his arms.
His own little dog
began to yap
with excitement.
Then Rory
snatched up her blanket from the
wheelchair and tossed that
overboard, too.

"The girl's gorn mad!" cried Aunt
Awful. "Grab 'er, Barnaby!"

Uncle Buckup caught hold of the
sash round Rory's waist
as she clambered
awkwardly on to the
rail.

"Jump!" shouted the
boy.

Rory swiped at Uncle

18

Buckup with her crutch and heard a ripping sound as the sash tore away. Again she struck out so that he had to snatch the crutch from her hand to protect himself. At that moment she half-jumped, half-fell into the darkening water.

"Help! Do something, Barnaby!" cried Aunt Smoother.

"What can I do?" he yelled back. "I can't swim, can I?"

"Nor can't she!" screeched Aunt Awful. "Save her, somebody!"

Then suddenly the lamp was out and the boy was in the water. He grabbed the struggling Rory by the collar and heaved. Her long wet dress made her heavy and her flailing arms battered him about the head, but grimly he hung on as he hoisted himself back on to his boat. For such a skinny young ragamuffin he was tough, but it took him all his strength to pull the girl aboard, too. "Hang on to your drawers, Droops!" he panted and with one last heave, he dragged her to safety.

He managed to sit her, spluttering, on the stern seat with Jim in her wet lap and get her blanket across her shoulders. The boat rocked alarmingly as he got himself into position to manage the oars. "Will you row or shall I, madam?" he enquired with a grin.

"I can't. I don't know how," she said, ashamed.

"What's happening?" came voices from overhead. "Where is she?"

"PERLEEEECE!" screamed Aunt Awful.

"Blimey!" the boy whispered back. "Can't swim, can't row. Who are you? A fine lady or something?"

"There's nothing fine about me," muttered Rory through chattering teeth. "But please, get a shift on!"

"Oh, please, is it?" said the boy. "That ain't a word we often hear. We'll row for a please, won't we, Rats?"

The oars dug deep and they were away.

Homeward Bound

They didn't speak for a while. Now
and then Jim whimpered, and
snuggled up to Rats as if they had
been chums for life. Now that her
teeth had stopped chattering from
the shock, Rory felt curiously warm.

As they came round a bend, the
rushes on the riverbank and the
dark overhanging willows began to
thin out. Rory could see lights
ahead and hear beery voices.

"That's the Chain and Anchor," said the boy. "There's a merry lot in tonight."

They passed more tall tarry buildings with slipways down to the water where Dutch barges waited, their red sails hanging limp. The moon was up now and Rory could see pulleys and chains dangling from doorways in the upper floors. "Wharfs," said the boy. "Can you smell the baccy and the rum? It ain't far now to my place."

"Are we going to your house?"

"House? Shack, more like. But I dunno where else to take you," said the boy. "Is that all right with you, your ladyship?"

"Don't," said Rory. "I'm nothing.

I've only one leg, and I've no mother or father."

"Nuffink!" cried the boy indignantly. "Nobody's nuffink! Even orphans like us."

"Then you're an orphan, too."

"Yeah. So we're two peas in a pod, us two, and we ain't even been introduced. Roland Handy's my name or Rollo for short. What's your handle?"

"Aurora. But I prefer Rory."

"Two Rs!" said Rollo gleefully. "Like in terrific!"

"I'm afraid I'm not much good at reading," said Rory. "I've only just started."

"Garn!" said Rollo. "You said you couldn't swim but that didn't stop

you jumpin' in the water, did it?
That makes you terrific. Anyway, I'll
teach you reading if you like. I've
got a book indoors. And here we
are, look. 'Ome."

The Crow's Nest

"'Ome" was a mud-coloured cabin with a stout front door made of planks. The curving walls were a mixture of scraps – canvas sails and leather sewn together with the sides of tea-chests and painted over with tar. It had a sturdy framework of timbers and was battened down tightly with ships' ropes, set on a bank under some willow trees above a thin strip of beach, and

26

sheltered even more by the black wall of an ancient warehouse.

The boy made fast the boat and ran ahead. Both dogs leapt to join him, then dashed about wildly, barging into each other, having fun. Rory watched Rollo unlock the door and swing it wide. "Welcome to the Crow's Nest," he called.

"I … I don't think I can get there," said Rory. She hesitated, feeling at a loss. "I can't get across soft ground – not without my crutch. I …" Then, gulping in a deep breath, she changed her mind. "Wait! It's all right. I can crawl."

She had got about halfway up the beach with her blanket under her arm when the dogs ran up to urge her on. Then Rollo was by her side with a broom, a saw, a hammer, a strip of leather, and a mouthful of tacks. "Mo meed for that," he said gently, so as not to spit out the tacks. "Let's measure this up."

He held the handle of the broom to her shoulder and sawed a length off it in a trice. Then he pulled the leather tight and smooth over the head of the broom and tacked it neatly into place. "There," he said, slipping it under her arm. "That's you all shipshape and Bristol fashion!"

"Thank you," she said. "If only ..."

But how could she tell him that she didn't want a crutch, even this special one?

"Don't you worry," said Rollo, seeming to read her thoughts. "This is just for now. I'm Handy by name and handy by nature, me! If you like, I can measure you up proper and make you a leg later."

"What, a peg-leg like a pirate's!" said Rory with a laugh.

"Here! That's an idea," said Rollo, chuckling too. "You and me, a couple of pirates! That'd make a change from mudlarking! But no, it wouldn't be no peg-leg. I'd make you a proper job to match your other one."

Inside, with a candle lit, it was

warm and dry and snug. There was even furniture: two wooden chairs finished in leather, and a low table.

"Take a seat," said Rollo. "They're nice and steady. I made 'em meself."

"Did you really?" said Rory, impressed.

"You never go short of flotsam and jetsam round here," he said. "You'd be surprised what the old river chucks up!"

He set up a portable stove a little way from the front door. "Too smoky inside," he explained. "That's why I've made it so it packs away. It's got its own stove-pipe and everything. See how it opens right up? I got the idea from a telescope."

And up it went.

Soon the fire was lit and the kettle was dancing and steaming on the stove. They took their tea hot and sweetened with treacle out of proper china cups with saucers. "Found these the other day mudlarking just down-river from the Houses of Parliament!" Rollo declared. "Might have been the Prime Minister 'ad his tea out of these!"

"Will you take me mudlarking?" asked Rory.

"Got to," came the quick reply. "It's either that or both go 'ungry."

Rapid Fire

So Rory became an apprentice-mudlark.
She asked for a pair of trousers to
disguise herself and a hat to hide
her flaming hair. Rollo was happy to
part with his spare breeches and she
wasn't fussy about a few patches.

But first she had to learn how to
handle the boat, how to row, how
to use the current and a scrap of
sail to save energy. It took nerve to
weave among big sailing ships and

to dodge the lumbering barges. And all the time she had to keep an eye open for nosy police boats on the lookout for a redheaded runaway. She was a quick learner and she had unusually strong arms.

Soon, if Rollo spotted something interesting ashore, she could guide the boat exactly to the place he pointed to and ground it with hardly a jolt. Rollo would leap ashore with the dogs and together they dug fast, throwing up a mud storm behind them. Then Rollo would stoop and hold up … a candlestick, maybe, or a pocket-watch, a bowler hat, a coconut.

Every night after supper, by the light of the smoky lantern, Rollo taught Rory to read. His book was about an orphan called Oliver Twist. It was full of long hard words, but so brave and full of adventures that Rory was eager to get quicker so that she could hurry the story along. One night she managed to read the word "impeccable".

"I think that's my favourite word so far," she said dreamily. "Do you think you could make me an impeccable leg?"

"I'll 'ave a go," said Rollo. "Let me 'ave a good think about how to do it."

Next day he steered them to one of his favourite hunting grounds along the Limehouse shoreline. After a heavy rain, when the river ran fast, all sorts of things began to appear in the shifting sands and slime.

It was a lucky day. First Rollo dug up a mouldy purse with a shilling, a sixpenny piece, three halfpennies and a farthing in it. He put that in his pocket and turned to something else that was sticking out of the mud. It was something shiny and varnished, made of wood. And it was stuck fast.

Suddenly a crowd of wild, ragged children appeared like rats, led by an older boy with a clay pipe clamped between his rotten teeth. His top hat was tilted cockily to one side.

"It's Black Jack's crew!" cried Rollo. "Stand by to repel boarders!"

They charged at Rollo, howling a war-cry, the big boy swinging a length of knotted rope like a cutlass.

The dogs were soon at their ankles, making them hop and squeal, but the big lad was closing in fast on Rollo. "Giss that purse or I'll bash your brains in!" he growled.

Rollo was still tugging at the wooden thing as the boy got close enough to batter him. "You've asked for it!" Black Jack shouted and swung his weapon – but at that very moment, a great gob of mud hit him right in the eye!

"Good shot, Rory!" cried Rollo. "Rapid fire, now!"

Then Rory really let fly. The bully tried to cover his face and head as mud cannon-balls rained down on him and his crew. With a final heave, Rollo got the varnished bit of wood clear of the mud and clobbered his attacker on the knee with it, making him howl and drop his rope. More well-aimed shots found their mark and the whole gang turned to run for it.

In the excitement, Rory's cap had flown off and her red hair had sprung loose. Out of range now, the boy with the pipe stopped and pointed at her. "It's that missing girl!" he yelled. "There's twenty guineas reward for findin' her!"

The Impeccable Leg

As they rowed homeward, Rory was anxious to know about Black Jack. Rollo explained that Black Jack was a crook a bit like Fagin in the story they were reading about Oliver Twist. Only instead of teaching his crew to pick pockets, Black Jack trained them to spy on poor unsuspecting mudlarks and rob them of any valuables they found.

"We shall have to keep a sharp

lookout for him and his thievin'
mob! I don't think they'll venture
down Putney way, though. We
should be safe there."

Rory dug the oars in deeper and
pulled with quicker, worried strokes,
but she soon cheered up when she
saw the grin on Rollo's face. "My
word, what you just done was
'andsome!" he cried and the boat
rocked as he wiggled his backside
in delight. "That lummock would
have stole our purse if it wasn't for
you. And he'd have run off with
this."

"What is that, exactly?" asked
Rory.

"Why, ain't you never seen a
boot-tree

before?" Rollo asked back. "Talk about a slice of luck!"

What made it especially lucky was that the wooden foot that was made to keep an ankle-boot in shape was just Rory's size. And it was made for a right boot, not a left one.

As soon as they were safely back to the Crow's Nest, Rollo turned to with his carpenter's tools. It took long hours of patient work and experiments with different sorts of pads and straps before he was quite content with it.

"Oh my word! It's beautiful!" said Rory as she balanced herself on the finished article.

Her first steps were as clumsy

and faltering as a young foal's. "Oh, I shall never get the hang of walking!" she exclaimed as she fell flat for the tenth time. But with practice and encouragement, she got better.

"I would say that leg's impeccable," said Rollo. "Wouldn't you?"

"It is impeccable," agreed Rory. "And now I have it, I intend to make myself useful."

"As a pirate or a mudlark?" enquired Rollo.

"Both," came the answer.

An Astonishing Find

One stiflingly hot day, Rollo
reckoned it would be safe if they
took the boat up-river towards
Richmond. The air was fresh there
and he knew some shady walks
everyone would enjoy.

He and Rory were cooling their
toes in a stream when the dogs
started scrabbling under a hedge.
What they sniffed out was too
heavy for them to drag into the

daylight by themselves. Never mind: they both earned a butcher's sausage for supper that night.

Rollo and Rory laid out the contents of the bag by candlelight. "It's old," muttered Rollo as he ran his fingers along the long, broad barrel of a musket. "And it's well oiled. Must have belonged to a poacher. You'd have no trouble knocking down ducks or hares with a gun like this!"

"There's dry gunpowder in this horn, look," said Rory. "And flints in this rag."

"We'll clean 'er up," said Rollo,

beaming. "Then she'll be just the job for catching us a rabbit or two."

"Fishface!" protested Rory, with mock-horror. "You wouldn't, would you?"

"Only if I have to, Droopy Drawers!"

"Sauce!" shouted Rory with a scream of laughter and got his head in a headlock.

The sight of their master and mistress milling around like a couple of merry prize-fighters sent the dogs completely silly. Jim forgot himself completely, grabbed Rory's blanket and shook it. Rats got his teeth into the other end of the blanket and challenged Jim to a tug-of-war.

The ruckus rose to fever pitch until with a RRRRRRRRRIPPPPP! The blanket was torn in two.

A shocked silence followed. Rory was horrified. Her precious blanket, spoiled forever!

Rollo was the first to move. "What's this?" he said with a gasp, handing Rory a flat yellowish packet. "It must have been in the lining!"

With trembling fingers, Rory opened it and took out a folded piece of paper. "Help me read it," she said. So together they said the words.

To our beloved Aurora Hope, light of our lives.

Should it ever come to pass that you are reading this and neither of us is present to tell you more, know this: that you are loved and that everything we have belongs to you.

Take your key to the inn called the Admiral Hardy at Greenwich and ask to speak to our faithful friend, Captain Edwin Shingle. We have entrusted to his care something that we wish may bring you great happiness.

With our blessings

Yr ever affectionate Papa and Mama,

Captain and Mrs Christopher James Hope

Rory and Rollo knew that to journey to Greenwich would take them past Limehouse and might attract the attention of Black Jack and his crew. Still, in high spirits as they were, that was a risk they were prepared to take. They reckoned there would be so much river-traffic near the beach where they had fought The Battle of the Purse that they might slip by unnoticed.

But just above that beach was a sinister figure in a crumpled top hat with a clay pipe clamped between his teeth. He had a telescope to his eye. And he was thirsty – for revenge.

The Admiral Hardy

The Admiral Hardy was a coaching inn. A handsome place, though a sooty one, built of brick and timber.

"Oh, Lor! This is too posh for the likes of us," said Rory to Rollo, looking down at her ragged clothes. "Look at those fine ladies come up from Dover!"

"Steady as she goes!" said Rollo. "For we have proper business here, you and I." With that, he took a dog under each arm and led the way.

"Oy! You two! Out!" cried a sour-faced porter in a striped waistcoat and red breeches. He stepped out from behind his desk to take Rollo by the ear. When he saw the dogs' teeth, however, he decided against it.

"Good day to you, sir," said Rory.

"Kindly inform Captain Shingle that Miss Aurora Hope is come to pay her respects."

"I'll give you 'respects', you grubby little guttersnipe!" roared the porter.

"Just one moment, Jenkins!" A commanding voice rose in a cloud of cigar smoke from behind a newspaper.

The porter stepped back as the man rose from his armchair. "Oh, very good, captain. If they ain't intrudin' on you."

"Not at all," said the man, stepping forward on bandy legs and shaking the children's hands. He closed one eye and looked carefully at Rory. "Well, well," he exclaimed. "Your dear father, God rest his soul, warned me that you might drop in and surprise me one day. And by Jove, dressed as you are, you're the spitting image of the flame-haired boy I first went to sea with!" He bowed deeply. "Walter Shingle is at your service."

Rory introduced Rollo and then asked, "Please sir, will you read this?" She held out to him the letter from her parents.

"Jenkins, fetch three plates of chops and peas to my rooms," asked the man. He looked at the dogs panting under Rollo's arms, their pink tongues hanging down. "Make that five plates. Piping hot, mind, and don't spare the gravy!" He shepherded the children up the creaking oak stairs.

With a good meal inside them, talk came easily. The captain read the letter and nodded gravely as he heard of Rory's miserable upbringing, of her rescue by Rollo, and of what her guardians had told her about the death of her mama and papa.

"A bad business, by thunder," said the captain. "And it makes me very sad. For the last time I saw your dear people, they were setting sail for the East Indies with high hopes, and you a tiny bundle of a Hope in your mother's arms."

"Why go to the East Indies, captain?" asked Rollo.

"Ah well, they had affairs to attend to there," the captain explained. "They gave me to understand that this

might take a year or two and after that it was their desire to return to England to live in a fine home that Captain Hope had purchased just outside London."

Rory's heart skipped a beat. "Do you happen to know the name of that house, sir?" she ventured.

"I fear I do not," came the reply, "but the time has come to search the ditty box that your papa left in my keeping." He drew aside a curtain and dragged into view a sturdy wooden sea-chest, adding: "With regret, I must smash the lock, for I'm blessed if I know what's happened to the key."

"I do!" cried Rory, feeling for it on the chain around her neck.

In a trice, the lid of the chest creaked open on its brass hinges and revealed, among other things: a naval officer's uniform, neatly folded; a pair of pistols; a sword with belt and scabbard; a brass telescope and a sextant in a leather case.

"These must be charts," said Rollo, eagerly unrolling a bundle of them and spreading them out on the floor. As he did so, out sprang some papers wrapped in red ribbon. They were covered in fine copperplate handwriting and sealed with wax.

"May I see those?" asked the captain, and in a moment he let out a whoop of delight. "Bless my soul!

These are legal documents signed by your father. This one is the deed for a plantation in the Indies and these are a bill of sale from a Lady Ailing, together with the deeds, signed over by her to your father, to Ailing House."

"Cor! Does that mean …?" exclaimed Rollo.

"It means that since Aurora's parents left everything to her, she may now consider herself a very wealthy young person!"

The Great Battle

Perhaps it wasn't terribly wise for
the children to return to the Crow's
Nest by water. But Rollo was keen
to wear the smart naval uniform that
Rory had given him as a reward for
his kindness and she had not the
heart to deny him the pleasure. He
sat in the stern, grand as could be,
his hand on the gold-plated hilt of
the sword in its scabbard, sometimes
putting the sextant or the telescope

to his eye in an important manner. Rory was so tickled by his ridiculous antics that she didn't notice the sleek six-oar jolly-boat slide out from Limehouse Creek. Six wild ruffians bent to the oars, urged along by a tall boy in a top hat and with a flintlock pistol in his hand. "Oh no! It's Black Jack!" she gasped when at last it caught her eye. "He's on to us, Fish!"

"Not if I can help it," said Rollo grimly. "Pull for your life, Droops!" With that, he threw himself on to his knees and drew out from his canvas bag the gleaming poacher's rifle. The wind was up and the water choppy, so by the time the wad was rammed home against a round lead ball, Black Jack's crew was so close that his strident voice could easily be heard.

"Stand and deliver the girl, or we'll cut you in two and sink you!" came the call.

"Keep rowing!" muttered Rollo, lying down on his belly and lowering the barrel of the musket on to the stern plate.

"But you've never fired that thing before!" said Rory, reseating herself and gathering the dogs beneath her to protect them.

"I'm goin' to sink that boat from underneath 'em, you just watch–"

The explosion was deafening. The dogs yelped, Rory screamed and the kick of the gun sent the boy sprawling into the arms of his shipmate. A cloud of choking smoke hid everything from view.

When it cleared, it was plain to see that a hole the size of a fist had appeared below the waterline in the bow of the jolly-boat that was almost close enough to ram them. As the river poured in to wet their feet, the rowers, already panicked by gunfire, flung themselves into the water. This set the vessel tossing so violently that the movement pitched their black-hearted boss backwards

overboard. He just had time to
shout a curse, then he was
swallowed by the waves.

Handy's Impeccable Emporium

Some years later, there was a knock on the door of Mrs Aurora Handy's magnificent drawing room. She clutched the silk skirt of her splendid peach-coloured dress with one hand and opened the door with the other. In doing so, she admitted a stout bow-legged gentleman upon whose broad shoulders sat a flame-haired baby boy. The baby laughed as he clung with both hands to the thick grey hair on the gentleman's head.

"Don't tire out your Uncle Shingle, dear!" cried Mrs Handy.

Mr Roland Handy was, at this moment, locking the door of Handy's Impeccable Emporium. His splendid department store in Oxford Street was famous the world over for its design of helpful gadgets. If you needed a machine to beat your carpet – or perhaps, a wonderfully comfortable wooden arm or leg – then Handy's was the only place to go.

"Message from the houseboat from Mrs Blaggard to thank you for the paint and varnish," announced old Captain Shingle with a wink.

Uncle Buckup and Aunt Smoother had packed up and gone,

but Aunt Awful was afraid that nobody else would employ an old misery like her. She had promised to keep a civil tongue in her head if she could just be allowed to stay on as cook.

"Bless you, madam," said Aunt Awful as she set down a plate of scones, "I always said you'd turn out lovely, didn't I?"

"I thought you said I was useless and should come to a bad end," murmured Aurora, but only to herself.

After all, now it didn't bother her one bit.